Thomas Rescues the Diesels

Based on *The Railway Series* by the Rev. W. Awdry

EGMONT

It was a busy time on the Island of Sodor. The Fat Controller asked Thomas to help Mavis finish an important job at the Quarry.

"I wonder why they sent you," Diesel said to Thomas. "Everyone knows that diesels are better workers," he added.

Thomas thought he was very rude.

Diesel played tricks on Thomas. He pushed him under a hopper so he got covered in dust. Thomas was shocked.

For the rest of the day, Diesel said rude things about steam engines and called Thomas a silly steamie.

Thomas wished he could show Diesel that steam engines are just as good as diesels.

The next day, Salty brought new fuel for the diesels. Mavis and Diesel were very excited.

"No new fuel for you, Thomas," said Diesel, nastily. "You just get dirty old coal!"

Thomas wished Diesel would stop being so mean to him.

Diesel started bragging as soon as he had been re-fuelled.

"I'm the fastest engine in the world!" he shouted.

Thomas tried to ignore him. But suddenly, Diesel went quiet.

"Oh!" he cried out a second later. "I feel strange. Something's wrong!"

Black smoke poured from Diesel and Mavis' engines.

"I feel sick!" wheezed Mavis.

"So do I!" groaned Diesel.

The Quarry Master came to see what was wrong with the diesels.

"It must be the new fuel," he said. "Some water must have leaked into the tanks!"

The diesels had all filled up with the new fuel and now they were all breaking down. Even Salty, who had brought the fuel, had been re-fuelled with it.

"Oh, dear!" he said. "We need help!"

The Quarry Manager told Thomas to collect fresh fuel from the depot.

"Right away, Sir!" said Thomas, and he quickly steamed away.

Thomas raced to the depot.

"I need all the clean fuel you've got. This is an emergency!" he said, urgently.

Workmen quickly loaded up fuel barrels on a wagon. It was heavy, so Thomas knew he would have to work hard to push it along the tracks.

Thomas puffed around the Island, taking fresh fuel to all the diesels.

Bert and 'Arry were pleased to see him. They felt better as soon as they had been given the clean diesel.

"Good work, Thomas," they said, happily.

Thomas set off again to deliver the fuel to the rest of the diesels.

Everyone cheered when Thomas arrived at the Quarry. Clean fuel was soon given to all the diesels.

"That's better," sighed Diesel.

"Thank you, Thomas," said Mavis.

Diesel helped Mavis and Thomas finish the important job on time.

The Fat Controller was delighted. "Thomas, you have rescued the diesels!" he said. "You are a Really Useful Engine."

Thomas smiled happily and even Diesel agreed that a steamie had saved the day!